A Note to Parents and Caregivers:

Read-it! Readers are for children who are just starting on the amazing road to reading. These beautiful books support both the acquisition of reading skills and the love of books.

 The PURPLE LEVEL presents basic topics and objects using high frequency words and simple language patterns.

 The RED LEVEL presents familiar topics using common words and repeating sentence patterns.

 The BLUE LEVEL presents new ideas using a larger vocabulary and varied sentence structure.

 The YELLOW LEVEL presents more challenging ideas, a broad vocabulary, and wide variety in sentence structure.

 The GREEN LEVEL presents more complex ideas, an extended vocabulary range, and expanded language structures.

 The ORANGE LEVEL presents a wide range of ideas and concepts using challenging vocabulary and complex language structures.

When sharing a book with your child, read in short stretches, pausing often to talk about the pictures. Have your child turn the pages and point to the pictures and familiar words. And be sure to reread favorite stories or parts of stories.

There is no right or wrong way to share books with children. Find time to read with your child, and pass on the legacy of literacy.

Adria F. Klein, Ph.D.
Professor Emeritus
California State University
San Bernardino, California

For my flyboy, Rick—J.K.

Editor: Christianne Jones
Designer: Amy Bailey Muehlenhardt
Page Production: Melissa Kes
Creative Director: Keith Griffin
Editorial Director: Carol Jones
The illustrations in this book were created in watercolor and pen.

Picture Window Books
5115 Excelsior Boulevard
Suite 232
Minneapolis, MN 55416
877-845-8392
www.picturewindowbooks.com

Printed in the United States of America.

Library of Congress Cataloging-in-Publication Data
Kalz, Jill.
Flying with Oliver / by Jill Kalz ; illustrated by Benton Mahan.
p. cm. — (Read-it! readers)
Summary: Oliver takes a high flying adventure in his airplane as he tips, spins, and
bounces on clouds.
ISBN 1-4048-1583-X (hardcover)
[1. Flight—Fiction. 2. Airplanes—Fiction.] I. Mahan, Ben, ill. II. Title. III. Series.

PZ7.K12655Fly 2005
[E]—dc22
                                                          2005021446

Flying with Oliver

by Jill Kalz
illustrated by Benton Mahan

Special thanks to our advisers for their expertise:

Adria F. Klein, Ph.D.
Professor Emeritus, California State University
San Bernardino, California

Susan Kesselring, M.A.
Literacy Educator
Rosemount–Apple Valley–Eagan (Minnesota) School District

PICTURE WINDOW BOOKS
Minneapolis, Minnesota

Oliver loves to fly airplanes. Lots of his dreams come true when he flies.

He nudges the stick. The airplane takes off.

Oliver twitches his thumb. The
airplane tips on its side.

He flips a switch. The airplane starts to let out smoke.

Oliver wiggles his finger. The airplane soars higher.

It makes a big
loop-dee-loop.

O is for Oliver!

16

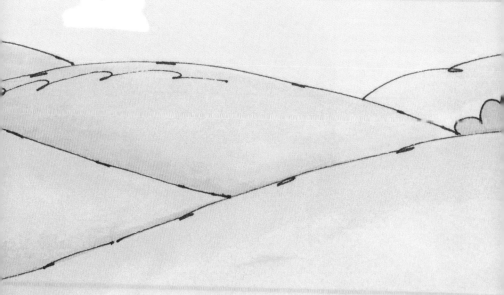

He swats at a bug. The airplane
bounces on the clouds.

Oliver sneezes. The airplane spins
like a pinwheel.

He winks and whistles. A dream
comes true. The airplane scoops him
up on its wing.

21

Who knows where Oliver and his airplane will go?

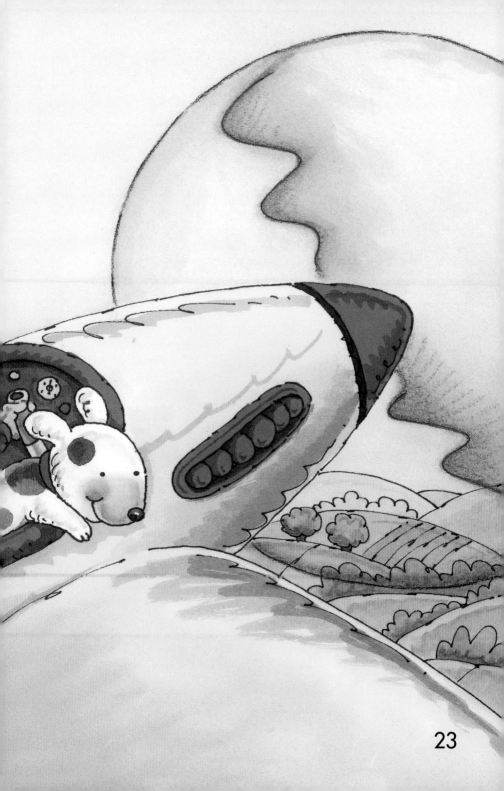

23

More *Read-it!* Readers

Bright pictures and fun stories help you practice your reading skills. Look for more books at your level.

At the Beach 1-4048-0651-2
Bears on Ice 1-4048-1577-5
The Bossy Rooster 1-4048-0051-4
Dust Bunnies 1-4048-1168-0
Frog Pajama Party 1-4048-1170-2
Jack's Party 1-4048-0060-3
The Lifeguard 1-4048-1584-8
The Playground Snake 1-4048-0556-7
Recycled! 1-4048-0068-9
Robin's New Glasses 1-4048-1587-2
The Sassy Monkey 1-4048-0058-1
Tuckerbean 1-4048-1591-0
What's Bugging Pamela? 1-4048-1189-3

Looking for a specific title or level? A complete list of *Read-it!* Readers is available on our Web site:
www.picturewindowbooks.com